Dear Milli

I hope

enjoy th

Love Hilary

GW00866710

Fairy Ballerina Tales

By Hilary Thomas

To all the students I have had the honour to teach and who have in turn taught me so much.

Chapter One

Ruby the Fairy Ballerina

Ruby lived at the bottom of a beautiful, old oak tree a few fairy flutters from the sea in the middle of the bustling village of Faylinn. The door to her home had a heart carved into it, right in the middle. It was a house full of love, happiness and fairy dust!

Ruby loved her family. There was mummy – Alexandrite, Lexa for short. Lexa was the Fairy Queen's personal assistant and more often than not wore purple from top to toe. Lexa was always very busy but always made time for a cuddle and a bedtime story. Daddy – Jasper was a famous sculptor. He could usually be found creating amazingly lifelike models of the Fairy Queen and other famous fairies in his workshop at the back of the tree. Nanny Pearl was Ruby's grandmother, an ex-ballerina who was Ruby's biggest fan and spoilt her rotten at every opportunity. And finally there was Prince Florimund the rather smelly but very wonderfully licky dog.

More than anything in the world Ruby loved to dance but not just any type of dancing. Ruby loved **ballet!** She danced anywhere there was space and even when there wasn't, getting the occasional bruise in the process, but she didn't care, she just couldn't stop. She would dance around the kitchen table and even jump off the sofa imagining herself on stage in the most beautiful tutu diving into the arms of her Fairy Prince as he caught her amazingly elegant flying leap.

"Sit still little shuffle bottom" chastised Lexa gently. "I need to put two more pins in your bun. There, all done, now where's my wand and I'll add a little sparkle."

Lexa picked up her delicate, sparkling wand with a glistening, rainbow like jewel on top. Ruby yearned for one just like it even though she loved her pink standard issue training wand. It had pink satin ribbons tied round it. There was no doubt it was pretty but all trainee fairies had the same. There were three colours to choose from, pink, yellow or green. Ruby wanted a colour to match her ballet shoes so chose pink. A rainbow jewel was most little fairy's dream. They were very rare and had extremely powerful magic in them. Once a trainee fairy had passed all his or her magical exams they could choose any wand they most desired. Ruby was only eight years old. Another eight years of study were necessary before she could choose her very own wand.

Lexa raised her hand gently and said "Diamonds around the bun please" and waived it carefully over Ruby's head. From nowhere appeared a ribbon of diamonds dancing in the air that dropped down and placed themselves perfectly around Ruby's bun. "Stay on tight, with all your might." She added with a determined smile and nod of the head. And with that Ruby was ready for her ballet class.

Ruby rushed to the front door, grabbed her ballet bag and wand and shouted. "Hurry mum, I'd like to get there early to practice, they're choosing the parts for the show next week and we find out what ballet we are doing today. Hurry, hurry!"

"Nanny Pearl is taking you today Ruby." Lexa replied, "I have to go and help the Fairy Queen plan next year's summer ball. She's getting very stressed out and I need to make sure she's happy with the colour scheme. She can't decide whether to choose Forest Glade or Seaside Sanctuary. Good luck my darling, I'll be back for bedtime!"

Flash! Pop! **Ping**!

"Argh!" Screamed Ruby, "Nanny, I wish you wouldn't do that!"

Nanny had suddenly appeared right next to Ruby, waving her wand and smiling, oblivious to Ruby's fright.

"Ah when I was young and on stage! Did I tell you about the time when...." Said Nanny standing by the door staring off in the distance.
"Tell me on the way please Nanny, I must warm up properly" Ruby interrupted but gave Nanny a kiss on the cheek to say sorry but still hurry up.

"Of course my little fairy ballerina." Nanny Pearl replied fondly and with a swish of her wand, and a flutter of their wings they were in the air flying faster than the air speed limit (yes there is one for all fairies!) straight towards the Hilaria Tiptoes School of Ballet for budding ballerinas.

Chapter Two

Hilaria Tiptoes School of Ballet

"Darling! Great to see you!"

"Oh darling you look marvellous!

"You look fabulous darling, are those gossamer wing extensions?"

"Let's chat over dewcups and fairy cakes darling!"

As Ruby put on her ballet shoes and flew up to check her hair in the just out of tip toe reach mirror. She could hear the chatter of the parents and grandparents outside. You would think the summer holidays had been a year long rather than six weeks, they were noisier than all the young fairies put together. If she heard the word darling one more time she would..., she would..., err..., well she wasn't quite sure what she would do but it was VERY annoying!

Ruby rushed into the ballet studio. It was lined with mirrors and ballet barres. There were beautifully painted flowers and butterflies on the wall and all around the top of the room were what looked like strings and strings of fairy lights twinkling. But if you bothered to look a little more closely you would see that they were in fact hundreds of brightly shining fireflies waking up from their daytime nap. The fireflies lit up the ballet studios every evening allowing the fairies to dance way into the night.

Ruby's favourite poster of Francesca Houseflower and Steven McSunbeam from the Royal Ethereal Ballet was on the wall nearest the door. The ballet dancers were in the most exquisite pose. Ruby could stare at it for days but today she rushed past and started to warm up.

Next door she could hear a familiar sound. It was the music from the wand dance she had learnt when she was younger. She smiled to herself as she danced it one more time in her imagination.

"Hey hey, Roobs!" Shouted Flint as he ran into the room and sat down next to Ruby. "So great to see you. What do you think the show is going to be this year? Cinderella? The Nutcracker? I love that one!"

Ruby's smile stretched from ear to ear when she saw Flint. He was one of her best friends and a brilliant dancer. He was always positive and enthusiastic. She couldn't help but be happy in his company. He lived next to the sea at the south of the village in a very modern *imported* palm tree.

"Hi Flint, hmmm, let me think" pondered Ruby. She thought for a little while and then said "to be honest anything where I get a part. The older fairies are going to get the main roles but I hope I get to do something fun and wear a great costume." Secretly she was hoping for a good part to show off her dancing. She loved performing on stage but she was only young and she knew the older children would dance all the main parts.

Before they could continue their conversation in flew the other students including Coral, Ruby and Flint's other best friend. Coral could sometimes be a little shy and was good at worrying but she was a fun and kind friend both Flint and Ruby adored. Coral lived four trees away from Ruby in a white birch tree next to the cricket ground. Ruby met Coral when they were babies at the local fairy playgroup. Coral had prodded Ruby in the arm and laughed. Ruby had giggled and that was it. Best friends for life! Coral's favourite colour was orange. She had the prettiest orange ballet outfit for class with a matching white and orange flower in her hair.

All the ballet students said hello to each other, some hugged and shared their summer holiday stories, others just flew around the studio excitedly, as that is what excitable fairies tend to do. They have wings you see, and they rather like using them. Wouldn't you?

There was an air of anticipation as the fairies listened to a familiar, beautiful melody drifting down the corridor towards the studio. The melodious sound grew nearer and nearer. The studio door creaked open and in floated a celesta (a small piano with metal keys that makes soft heavenly sounds), an oboe and a violin. The dancing, playful instruments entered the room and began spinning in the air playing the Dance of the Sugar Plum Fairy music from The Nutcracker ballet.

After circling the studio once the instruments came to a halt, mid-air, hovering as if waiting for something, the beautiful melody playing on.

POP!

A sudden explosion of glitter and the owner of the school, Hilaria Tiptoes appeared in the centre of the room. She was accompanied by darting damselflies and hovering hummingbirds. They swarmed around Hilaria dancing in time to the music as she spun round and round as the music started to fade. She clapped her hands and off the creatures flew towards the walls and joined the painted flowers and butterflies that decorated the classroom. As Hilaria moved off towards her students she left a trail of rainbow sparkles that dispersed as soon as she landed on the tip of her toe.

Hilaria gently lowered into first position (a ballet position where you stand with your heels together and your toes turned to the sides evenly). The music finally stopped and the instruments floated over to the corner of the studio and waited for their next instructions.

Hilaria had wings that shone brightly like stars in the night sky and her wand had golden ribbons trailing beneath a pale pink glistening jewel. She had danced on stage when she was young and just loved teaching the fairies everything she knew. Always full of energy and ideas, Hilaria made class a happy place to be.

Although she could be a little bit bossy and was VERY fussy about good ballet technique but she was NEVER mean or cruel.

"Welcome back!" She boomed cheerily. "I hope you all had a superb summer break. I certainly did but now it's time for hard work and practice to get ready for our show. The show we will be putting on this year is..." She smiled and paused for dramatic effect. The children huddled together clutching each other with great excitement.

"The show will be..... Alice in Wonderland! Auditions start next week!" There was a cheer and lots of excitable chatter until Hilaria said.

"Take your places at the barre please."

Chapter Three

Auditions

The ballet school was a flutter of fidgety fairies of all ages waiting to try out for the roles in Alice in Wonderland! Ruby and Coral had their faces squashed up against the small window of Studio One, where the oldest fairies were dancing and acting. They were auditioning for the role of Alice and their faces were full of wonder and astonishment as they acted out a scene from the ballet. Ruby was terribly impressed. There were jetés and sautés (leaps and jumps) and the most beautiful port de bras (movement of arms). Ruby and Coral couldn't decide who they liked the best.

"Opal is so elegant!" Said Coral. "But Amber is a brilliant actress. Glad I'm not choosing."
"Look at Amethyst, she can do box splits and everything!" Gawped Ruby. Ruby had been trying to do the box splits for ages. That's the position where you sit on the floor and try and make your legs go straight out to the left and right in a line. It is extremely difficult. Ruby was so close, if only she was allowed to use magic, but no, that was strictly forbidden in

ballet. She grumpily accepted that she had to be patient and practice carefully as she'd been taught.

"Children it's time! It's your turn to audition. How glorious!" Shrieked Nanny Pearl, clasping her hands together and spinning around looking more excited than the two girls could ever possibly be.

"Oh!" Coral panicked for a moment and wondered whether she really wanted to do this. "I'm, I'm not sure." She mumbled.

At that very moment as if reading Coral's mind, Hilaria flew in.

"Are you ready my beautiful Fairy Ballerinas?" she said gently. "Please remember that everyone has a part in the ballet. All you are really doing is helping with some new steps I've made up for each character. It would be a great help if you could try them for me."

This calmed down Coral quite considerably. Ruby rushed past them both into the studio shouting "come on let's go!" Hilaria and Coral looked at each other, rolled their eyes and laughed. This was going to be fun.

"Are you warmed up?" Asked Hilaria.
The two girls nodded and gulped.

"Glissade, glissade, sissonne, pas de chat." Hilaria sung the ballet steps to the music she wanted the children to dance. It had taken them quite a while to learn the names of the ballet steps over the years as they were all in a different language. Hilaria explained to all new students "French is the language of ballet, my poppets, we must learn all the names of the steps; the whole universe teaches ballet in French!"

As Ruby and Coral danced they began to realise what part they were dancing. They had to hold an oversized pocket watch and rush about in a panic. Can you guess what part it was? Ruby definitely could. After a while Ruby said.

"Excuse me Hilaria, but if I am not mistaken these steps are what the White Rabbit might dance!" Ruby and Coral's eyes were wide with excitement.

"I didn't think it would take you long to guess" said Hilaria "You two are very special dancers and I would like you both to learn the role of the White Rabbit. We have two performances in one day and it is a very big part so I would like you Coral to dance in the morning show and you Ruby to perform the role in the afternoon show."

Both girls squealed with delight and ran over and hugged Hilaria so hard she had to steady herself with her wings in order not to fall over.

"I am trusting you with the great responsibility of learning all the steps and performing them throughout the whole ballet." Hilaria continued shaking out her squashed wings. "I have faith in you but you must work very hard for me. Flint will be your understudy." She informed them. "But he has another role too. He will be The Knave of Hearts, the naughty one who stole the jam tarts."

♡

Chapter Four

RooRoo Bunny

Christmas holidays were only a few jingle bells away. Lexa was working hard as usual and was up at the palace helping decide on the menu for the Fairy Queen's Christmas Eve party. The Queen was struggling to choose between two dessert dishes. Strawberry Sparkle Surprise - the surprise being that strawberry soufflé blows up almost hitting the ceiling then gently floats down landing into crystal dishes in front of each guest with a lit sparkler and a cherry on top! The other option was a Christmas Bomb Cake. As you can imagine it looked like a large, round cartoon bomb with a fuse on. Once lit it took four seconds before it blew up sending cake splatting into everyone's face. Guests would have to eat the cake off their own faces. Lexa wondered whether this would be too much, even with an instant clean-up spell.

Lexa had been away more than at home. Ruby missed her very much but today Ruby was happily skipping around her father's workshop pointing her wand at his tools and making them perform a ballet in the air as she hummed Swandhilda's solo from Coppélia.

On this day Jasper was carving a huge marble statue of a ballet dancer, it looked like a big lump of stone because he had only just begun.

"Daddy?" Said Ruby

"Yes RooRoo Bunny" Jasper replied. Ruby was glad no one else heard her dad call her RooRoo Bunny. It was embarrassing!

"Who are you creating this week?" She asked this every time her dad had a new lump of rock delivered. The last one was of the Fairy Queen and was especially made for her birthday.

"Ahh, I was hoping you would ask," he said, "it's Steven McSunbeam the famous ballet dancer who dances for the Royal Ethereal Ballet. The Fairy Queen has asked for the statue to be made to celebrate Fairy Ballet Day and we are meeting up at the castle to talk about it. Steven will be there too.

"What...... Who..... When....?" Ruby screamed and flew around the room shrieking. "Can I come, can I come, can I come? I have to come with you! Please Daddy please!"

Ruby couldn't contain her excitement, there was a popping sound like a party popper being pulled and out of her ears shot clouds of glitter that raced around the room and briefly formed the outline of a ballet dancer and several heart shapes circling it. It disappeared into thin air. When Ruby was excited glitter always popped out of her ears. Fairies are funny little things aren't they!

"Well now young RooRoo Bunny Pie," Jasper smiled "Nanny Pearl is away and there is no one to look after you at home so you have to come up with mum and I. But you will only meet him to say hello, then you'll have to go off to mum's office."

Ruby had completely forgotten about the tools in the air. They dropped back into the tool box with an almighty clatter. Jasper jumped at the noise but Ruby was completely oblivious, she had flown up to the top of the workshop and was performing summersaults as her ears popped out more glitter and the occasional fruity smelling glitter popped out of her bottom too! Oops!

Chapter Five

To The Palace

The morning of the trip to the palace arrived. Outside Ruby's window the robin who lived higher up in the tree was singing his morning melody. To fairies a robin's singing sounds just like an opera singer. He woke Ruby up every morning but today she was the one who woke first. She was stretching her legs and pointing and flexing her toes to warm up and strengthen her feet. The first task in Ruby's morning routine was to practice her "good toes, naughty toes" in bed before she got up. Ruby looked out of her bedroom window. "Good morning Mr Robin, today is going to be great adventure!" She said and waved over at the red breasted bird. He nodded at her and continued his song.

Prince Florimund trotted in to Ruby's bedroom and hinted that he wanted his breakfast. Well when I say hinted he squealed and barked at Ruby, then wagged his tail and galloped off towards the kitchen looking back at her making sure she was following. She dutifully obliged and poured out a large bowl of Bark Chips. He licked his lips and devoured them in seconds followed by a satisfied belch sending the smell of what he had just eaten right up Ruby's nose. She loved him dearly but goodness he was stinky! She coughed and held her breath as she watched him go through his doggy door to their back garden. He trotted off to deposit a whiffy, brown parcel at his favourite spot behind the hollyhocks.

Ruby raced back upstairs into her parents' bedroom, jumped on the bed then flew round and round shouting "today's the day! Get up, get up!"

Jasper covered his head with the pillow and groaned. Lexa sat up trying to open her still sleeping eyes. "Someone's excited! Good morning Ruby." Lexa yawned, gave Ruby the biggest hug and continued, "Time to get ready for our trip, go and choose what you want to wear."

At 9am all three were standing ready outside their home. Ruby was dressed her favourite green dress, which was, of course, extremely sparkly! Although they could fly themselves to the Palace with their own wings it was rather a long way and today was a special exception. They were going to be flown by the Fairy Queen's Osprey, a majestic bird of prey and a perfect long distance flyer. The Osprey's speedy flight was twice as fast as fairy flight and they arrived outside the palace with plenty of time to spare.

The palace was the most enormous building Ruby had ever seen. The vast walls were made of polished white marble. The only colours to be seen were the red and pink flags on the towers that flapped gently in the breeze. Once inside it was quite different. As soon as they walked through the huge front doors Ruby saw rainbows! The palace was filled with amazing colours from floor to ceiling. Sunlight shone through the elaborate, stained glass windows in the entrance hall adding an extra layer of magical colour. If Ruby had the time to it would take a week to explore the hundreds of rooms inside the Fairy Queen's home. Ruby's mouth was wide open in amazement as she walked through the building. She passed room after room until they reached an extremely elegant room that was purple and gold. A fairy was sitting on a purple sofa with his back to them. All Ruby could see was that he had red hair and a very straight back with golden wings. She knew immediately who it was and squeezed her parents' hands tightly. As they walked closer he stood up and turned around to greet them.

"Good morning Lexa, Jasper, good to see you both again. This must be your budding ballerina Ruby." He turned to Ruby and continued.

"I've heard so much about you, you are quite talented I hear." Ruby still had her mouth wide open but just in time she closed it, smiled shyly and replied, "not a wanna, Mr McSunbeam, er, oh I mean what an honour!" Ruby's eyes widened and she blushed with embarrassment, her cheeks turning as red at the jewel she was named after.

Steven smiled and pretended not to notice she had muddled her words. He continued "I have some tickets for you to come to The Royal Ethereal Ballet to watch Francesca Houseflower and I dance in Alice in Wonderland. It will be on straight after the unveiling of my statue. I believe you'll be dancing in this ballet for your school performance."

"Oh yes please, thank you, yes, thank you, that's wonderful, thank you, please, yes!" Ruby blurted out and curtsied, trying to control the glitter desperate to pop out of her ears.

Just then in flew the Fairy Queen. "Ahh you're all here, good, good." She starting talking terribly quickly, without seeming to take a breath. "Hello again Ruby, my goodness haven't you grown. Here are the table plans for the Kingdom dinner dance in March, Lexa. I'd like to discuss them after this meeting, if you could take Ruby to your office please. Jasper, Steven delightful to see you again, let's get down to business."

As soon as Ruby was in Lexa's office she flew up high, pirouetted and joyfully danced around the chandelier. This time she allowed her ears to pop!

Chapter Six

The Gift

It was finally Christmas Day, presents had been given, a sumptuous lunch eaten and Father Christmas's elves had finally gone. *Elves*? Yes, Elves. Several of Father Christmas's elves were invited for Christmas lunch every year to eat Nanny Pearl's deliciously, delectable delights. Elves *love* a fairy Christmas lunch and they deserve one after such hard work making all those marvellous presents, don't you think?

Nanny Pearl, who was sitting by the fire in her favourite rocking chair called Ruby over and handed her a small silver box. She held it carefully in her hand. It opened all by itself to reveal the most enchanting necklace. The pendant was a fairy ballerina in an arabesque (a balance - one leg lifted behind, one arm to the side and one in front, palms facing downwards). It was made out of white gold and the dancer had a tutu made of rubies.

Nanny Pearl bent over and whispered. "My darling, I was given this necklace by the Director of the Royal Ethereal Ballet, the divine Sir Kevin B'Unions. It was many years ago when I was still dancing. Now you are old enough to wear it, it is yours. A ruby for my Ruby. I love you my beautiful ballerina."

Ruby hugged and kissed her grandmother. Nanny Pearl picked up her wand and waved it over the necklace and chanted. "To a new owner now is best, gently around her neck to rest." The necklace rose gracefully in the air guided by Pearl's wand and settled around Ruby's neck comfortably as if it had always been there. Ruby smiled and gave her grandmother one more squeeze and she ran off to look at her precious gift in the mirror.

Chapter Seven

Rehearsal

"No that's not right! Five, six, seven, eight AND one…" Shouted Hilaria over the music.

The rehearsal had been going well until the Queen of Hearts' card soldiers fell over at the wrong part in the music. They were supposed for fall over, you see, to make the audience laugh but they kept falling over too early in the music, landing badly, splat on their bottoms and then giggling too much at their mistakes. Flint, Coral and Ruby were watching at the side of the room. Actually they weren't watching anymore. They were creased over hugging their tummies and stamping their feet because they were laughing so hard.

"That's quite enough, come on now let's take a five minute break to calm down. We need to get it right before we leave tonight. Go and get a drink of water." Hilaria said with a tired smile. She knew they could do it, they just needed to concentrate.

Flint flew over to his teacher. "Please could you watch my Knave of Hearts solo? I am a bit stuck on the timing of the pirouette."

While Flint was practicing with Hilaria, Ruby and Coral practiced their White Rabbit role in the corner of the room. They loved dancing it and couldn't wait to try on the costumes they had been measured for only a week earlier; surely they would be ready soon.

An hour later and the rehearsal was over. Hilaria was so pleased with her students' efforts that she picked up her wand and began to cast a spell. "Hard work was done today, let everyone know my delight. A chocolate reward wrapped in gold, for all to take home tonight." Everyone held out their hands and chocolate coins the size of saucers landed in their palms.

When she arrived home Ruby found Lexa and Jasper in the workshop organising the transportation of the now finished statue of Steven McSunbeam. Ruby had to admit that her father was a talented sculptor, the statue was a perfect likeness. He was in a princely pose with his balletic muscles rippling; his head held high and proud.

Lexa was reading from her schedule.

"Four unicorns from The Unicorn Transport Express will be here tomorrow at 7am. I need you to go with them and tell them exactly where to lower the statue so you are happy with it. And Jasper it looks fantastic, just like him."

Lexa paused briefly to smile proudly at Jasper. She continued. "Oh and Nanny Pearl and Ruby will be up at lunchtime with the others. Hi Ruby!" called Lexa when she noticed her daughter. "We're just sorting out tomorrow, Nanny Pearl is making buttercup dumplings for tea in the kitchen, your favourite."

Lexa was in major organising mode and Jasper looked as pleased as Prince Florimund when he had found his favourite bone under the sofa. That is pleased indeed, although luckily unlike Prince Florimund, Jasper didn't try to lick anyone's face! Ruby smiled and left them to it. She found Nanny Pearl singing in the kitchen stirring what was to be their evening meal in a large pot on the stove.

"Nearly ready, now for the secret ingredient," and she picked up her wand and waved it over the delicious smelling stew. "Made with love and time and care, with enough to eat and plenty to spare". And she dropped something into the stew and stirred it.

Once it was ready the whole family sat at the large round table in the kitchen and tucked into the stew making satisfied, yummy sounds as they devoured every last bit.

Chapter Eight

Grand Unveiling

"Left….*Left*….. a little more… and…. lower it. No, no! Not too quickly! Ah, yes… *yes slowly and……* that's it, done! Thank you unicorns, I am in your debt!" Jasper was very happy, he bowed to the four unicorns who were at that point still holding the rope clasped in their teeth that had helped them lift the statue in to the perfect position. It had been placed in front of the Royal Ethereal Ballet's main entrance on top of a large circular marble stone. It looked *spectacular* thought Jasper, "Now let's cover it up ready for the big unveil!"

By the time Lexa, Nanny Pearl, Ruby, Coral and Flint arrived at the Royal Ethereal Ballet Theatre it was time to unveil Jasper's marvellous creation. There were several hundred fairies crowded round ready to watch the ceremony. Jasper stood in front of the statue with Steven McSunBeam.

There was a…. **Flash!** Pop! **Ping**! And the Fairy Queen dressed head to toe in gold with Lexa by her side joined Jasper and the famous ballet dancer to unveil the statue.

"It is with great pleasure that I announce the commencement of Fairy Ballet Day. Our new Alice in Wonderland ballet production opens today and we celebrate with this splendid statue of Steven McSunbeam sculpted by the outstanding talent of Jasper Tourmaline." Said the Fairy Queen as everyone cheered and clapped. "Steven please unveil your statue." She ordered.

Steven chaîné'd (chaînés – sounds like shennay, they are continuous travelling turns) towards the statue, bowed a deep, dramatically, swooping bow and took the corner of the silk sheet covering the statue. He pulled it down to reveal... his bottom!? Yes you read it correctly. The statue was the wrong way round and the first thing that everyone saw was the back of the statue, and the statue's bottom was directly in line with the real dancer's face. His face, the actual Steven's face, blushed a little (he's never come face to face, well err face to bottom with his own bottom before) and he looked at the Fairy Queen and Jasper for guidance.

"I only left them for a moment! I'm terribly sorry! The unicorns, they must have turned it round when I wasn't looking, but why?" complained Jasper looking rather confused. In the distance there was a sound of horses or could it be unicorns neighing; it did sound very similar to laughter. Who knew unicorns were so naughty?

"Not to worry." The Fairy Queen giggled "I shall fix it." And she muttered a levitation spell that very slowly and carefully turned round the statue back to its original position.

Everyone cheered and laughed and it wasn't long before even Jasper saw the funny side. Ruby ran over to Jasper and gave him the biggest hug and whispered in his ear. "It's marvellous, I love you daddy and the bottom is a perfect likeness!" Cheeky indeed!

STEVEN McSUNBEAM

Chapter Nine

A Royal Performance

At last it was time to see the performance of Alice in Wonderland. Her precious ticket in hand, Ruby with family and friends just behind, walked towards the dress circle entrance. She showed her ticket to the usher who smiled and pointed her to the front row. Some of the best seats in the house. The seats were a deep red velvet with gold trim and decorated all over the walls and ceilings were extravagant gold patterns. Ruby thought it was truly magnificent. The theatre was full of noisy chattering but as the lights slowly dimmed everyone went silent. Only the light of the orchestra pit could be seen. (For those who don't know the orchestra pit is directly under and in front of the stage and musicians sit in there for the whole ballet creating the most awe inspiring music.) In flew the conductor Keon Truffles. His long flowing hair and wings glistened in the light. He raised his hands and nodded at the musicians, his arms dancing their own ballet just for the orchestra. The music began and Ruby couldn't help but squeal with delight. She turned to Flint and Coral who were grinning like Cheshire Cats and then settled down to watch the performance.

Up went the curtain and from the ceiling a shining round sun appeared, floated down towards the stage and positioned itself at the back of the stage in the scenery on a blue sky background. It lit up the stage with amazing effect. The audience clapped with delight and in danced Alice with her friends.

"My favourite was Alice. I want to be Francesca Houseflower. She is the best!" Ruby exclaimed after the performance had ended.
"She was amazing, I loved the Mad Hatter too and the Knave of Hearts. But the caterpillar was brilliant!" Flint answered undecidedly.
"It was delicious darlings!" Purred Nanny Pearl.
"I wish we were as good as them." Sighed Coral.
"One day you just might be." Jasper smiled encouragingly and continued. "Time for home and hot chocolate with marshmallows and choccy sprinkles all round!"

Chapter Ten

Could You Repeat That Please?

It was almost time, there were a few days to go before the Hilaria Tiptoes School of Ballet's performance of Alice in Wonderland. The weekly ballet classes and extra rehearsals for the ballet school show were well underway. All dances had been learned, all costumes had been made and tried on and the fairies were getting very excited. It was the day of dress rehearsal - the run through of the whole ballet in full costume, on the stage with lights and music but no audience. It helped the children get used to dancing on stage under bright lights and of dancing with all the school not just their class. It also helped Hilaria to work out any problems they might have so that they didn't happen on the day of the show.

"Ruby, Nanny's here, it's time to go to rehearsal. I've received a butterfly mail from Hilaria to ask you to come in extra early." Shouted Jasper. He was in the hall with Nanny Pearl.

"Really, I wonder why?" Ruby replied skipping towards Jasper and Nanny Pearl. "Maybe some changes to my dance."

"Let's go my little one, chop chop!" Said Nanny Pearl. She was smiling even more than usual, thought Ruby. Nanny looked terribly pleased about something. Ruby shrugged it off as Nanny being her usual bonkers self and set off to the ballet school.

They met Hilaria at the door of the school, which was unusual. She was normally inside getting ready or with other students.
"Fabulous, you are here!" She clasped her hands together and gave Nanny Pearl a hug. "Thanks Pearlie, come in, come in, we must talk."

Hilaria led them into her office. Ruby was confused. There was no one else in the building other than the three of them. What could she have to say? Ruby sat down and waited for the explanation.

"Amethyst, as you know, is dancing the part of Alice in the show with Opal being her understudy." Hilaria said. Ruby nodded, she knew this already. "Well, they have both been asked to perform next week with the Royal Ethereal Ballet with a view to joining them as apprentices in the autumn. It is a dream come true. I have to let them go."

"Wow!" Said Ruby but after thinking a little more she added "Oh but that's when our show is, oh no! Who is going to play Alice? The White Rabbit will look a bit weird dancing alone." Ruby screwed up her face looking worried and started biting her nails.

"That's why I have asked you here Ruby." Hilaria smiled. "I'd like you to dance the role of Alice and we need to get started immediately."

"What? I mean pardon, could you repeat that please?" Ruby asked not believing what she was hearing.

"I want you, Ruby." Hilaria repeated. "You are going to be Alice. You probably know the steps already as you have been rehearsing with Amethyst. Coral will dance the White Rabbit in both performances to cover you taking on this role. I know you can do it Ruby, we have five days to get you up to speed."

It was true, Ruby already knew the choreography but she needed time to perfect it. It was more advanced than she was used to. She didn't want to dance it badly and be laughed at. She looked at Hilaria with determined eyes and said. "Thank you for choosing me. It is a great honour. I would absolutely love to but I have so much to learn and to practice. Can we start now and can we practice every single day until the performance?"

Chapter Eleven

Dress Rehearsal Disaster?

Several hours of practice later and Ruby heard everyone begin to arrive for the dress rehearsal. Ruby was stretching in the studio thinking through all the new steps she'd learnt. She was eating a packet of Pansy Petals to keep her energy levels high. Ruby knew how important it was to feed herself well to keep strong. Next door fairies were chattering as they put on their costumes. Ruby smiled to herself as she listened.

"Help! Mum I forgot my ballet shoes! Oh no they are here in my bag"

"I need more glitter for my hair!" "Stop flying about, come and sit still"

"I am so excited daddy, did I tell you I was excited?" "No dear only ten times today!"

"I can't wait to see everyone in their costumes"

"I'm hungry!"

There was a knock on the door and Nanny Pearl came in with the Alice costume. It was far too big for Ruby. Amethyst was several years older and much taller too. Luckily Nanny's magic was advanced enough to alter it very quickly. Ruby put on the costume carefully and Nanny got to work.

"A little tuck here, a fold just there" Nanny whispered waving her wand and continued. "Ribbon shorter, hem higher, now for your hair… that's it!" After five minutes she was done. The costume now fitted Ruby like a glove.

"You can look in the mirror. Fly over and see." Nanny said with a satisfied look on her face.

Ruby looked into the mirror but didn't see Ruby anymore, she saw Alice.

Ruby headed to the stage where everyone was gathering to hear Hilaria explain what was going to happen at the dress rehearsal. As Ruby walked along the corridor there were whispers and gasps at the costume she was wearing. She didn't say a word and walked up into the wings and onto the stage and stood as she had been instructed to next to Hilaria.

"Hello everyone!" Hilaria shouted springing into the air and landing in a deep curtsey. "It's dress rehearsal time! I need to inform you that we have had some cast changes. Amethyst and Opal have the tremendous opportunity of dancing with the Royal Ethereal Ballet next week so as you can see by her costume Ruby is now playing Alice. She is perfect for the role so please support her all you can!"

The stage erupted in applause and Ruby was squashed and squeezed and patted on the back by all her friends and several she really didn't know at all.

Once the dancers were in their starting positions in the wings (at the sides of the stage), Hilaria clapped her hands and the music began. Coral and Flint gave Ruby the biggest hug and whispered "break a leg, but not really!" No one says good luck to ballet dancers, it is thought be bad luck so they say break a leg or toi toi toi! All rather silly if you ask me! Ruby nervously nodded and smiled and set off onto the stage to dance.

In the second act Alice meets the card soldiers, the Knave of Hearts and the Queen of Hearts who likes to get an axeman to chop everyone's head off. The Queen was being played by Amber, she was a super dancer and when not playing a murderous dictator had always been very supportive of Ruby.

When Flint, who was the Knave of Hearts, came in with the tray of tarts he had stolen, the Queen, was supposed to mime kick him in the bottom so that he falls over and drops the tarts of the floor. The only problem was on this occasion the Queen did kick him in the bottom very hard, and this sent him flying in the direction of Alice who was pushed right off the edge of the stage.

"Argh!" Screamed Ruby.

"No!" Shrieked Hilaria.

"Ouch!" Yelled Flint.

"Oops!" Shouted Amber.

Luckily fairies have wings and Ruby started flying just before she hit the ground. She lowered herself down gently and called out. "Nothing broken, everyone ok?"

Everyone called out that they weren't injured and Hilaria asked them to do the scene again.

"This is what dress rehearsals are all about. Making mistakes, averting disasters." Hilaria said positively. "Amber if you could try not to kick so hard this time we'd all appreciate it!" Amber nodded with a rather embarrassed smile on her face.

The rest of the rehearsal went without a hitch but Ruby still needed help on a couple of steps she just couldn't quite get right. She wondered whether she would ever dance them well enough! Ruby thought she needed more help and much more time. Could she really be as good at Alice as Amethyst? Was hard work and passion really enough to get her through?

Chapter Twelve

No More Ballet!

All week Ruby practiced either with Hilaria or with Nanny Pearl. Every day she felt more confident but she still struggled with her grand jeté (big split leap). Her shoulders would hunch or her back leg would bend when it was supposed to be straight or her arms would flap or her foot would turn in as she landed. Something always went wrong. She was simply getting too tired.

On the day before the show Ruby and Nanny were at the ballet school practicing. They had been practicing for an hour. Nanny Pearl suddenly stood up and wrapped herself in her stylish red coat.

"That's enough. Home for a bath. Time to give your body a rest, no more practicing!"
Ruby looked horrified. "But Nanny!" She whined.

"No that's it, you know it, you know the steps and now you must *rest*" Nanny said gently. "You need fuel. I will make stew with buttercup dumplings and then you must snuggle up with Prince Florimund and have a nap. No more ballet, my little one."

With a bit of a grumble Ruby packed up her ballet bag and they set off for the short flight home.

After her bath and deliciously, dumplingy lunch Ruby snuggled up next to Prince Florimund on their huge squishy sofa and allowed herself to relax. The dog's gentle snoring sent Ruby off into a deep sleep within minutes.

"Ruby, time to wake up, Ruby, I have a butterfly mail for you!" Whispered Lexa gently. Ruby had been asleep for two hours. Prince Florimund woke up first and licked Ruby's face. Ruby woke and looked up at Lexa, wiped her dog licked wet cheek, patted Prince Florimund and saw a dainty letter in the design of an Orange-tip butterfly. It flapped a little and opened in the air lowering itself into Ruby's hands. She started to read it.

Dear Ruby

Francesca and I heard you had been given the role of Alice in your show tomorrow. I am sure you will be a great success. Please find enclosed Francesca's Alice band that she wore for the performance you came to see. She thought you might want to wear it in your show.

Dance from the heart, reveal your inner light,
Great talent will shine through, your future is bright.

Enjoy every minute!
Toi toi toi!

Love
Steven McSunbeam

As soon as Ruby had finished reading her letter the Alice band appeared out of thin air in front of her and lowered itself on top of the letter. She delicately picked it up and rushed to the mirror to put it on. It fit perfectly! Ruby placed the headband carefully in her ballet bag and skipped into the kitchen for tea, her confidence well and truly restored.

Chapter Thirteen

Curious!

"Today's the day Mr Robin." Said Ruby. She was feeling very excited and positive. Ruby was using her bedroom window sill as a ballet barre to practice her demi pliés (bend and stretches) and rises. The robin looked at Ruby for a moment as she bobbed up and down at the window and then, as usual, the robin nodded and carried on singing.

After a hearty breakfast of daisy cakes and dandelion squash Ruby prepared her ballet bag for the show.

Ballet Bag List
Glitter
Tights
Ballet shoes
Hair pins and grips
♥ALICE BAND♥
Snacks – Pansy Petals, Yummy Honey Teasels
Drink – Fairy Dew Drops
Wand
More glitter just in case!

Bag ready, Ruby put on her bejewelled fairy necklace, admired it in the mirror and gave herself a pep talk. "Enjoy today Ruby!" She said to her reflection. "You can do it! Go out there and show them what you are made of!"

"Ruby poppet darling!" Shouted Lexa from the hallway. "Are you ready to go?"

Flash! Pop! **Ping!**

"Argh!" Screamed Lexa, "Nanny, I wish you wouldn't do that!"

Nanny had appeared very suddenly next to Lexa, waving her wand and smiling, as she often did.

"Oh gracious, did I make you jump Lexa?" said Nanny Pearl with a cheeky smile "Where's Ruby?"

"Here I am!" Ruby flew into the hallway, her ballet bag clutched with both hands. She was not going to forget her precious Alice band. "Do you mind if we walk today?" Asked Ruby "It's such a gorgeously, sunny day and we are going to be inside for the rest of it!"

"How novel! Glorious idea!" exclaimed Nanny Pearl and off they set on foot giving their wings a well-earned rest.

The morning air was fresh and there was a soft breeze from the nearby sea. The grass beneath their feet was still moist with dew and the sun's gentle heat hugged the three fairies as they walked along to school chatting about the day to come. As they reached their destination Ruby saw the back of two people she thought she recognised walking a few metres away towards the nearby shops. One had red hair and the other dark brown. Curious! They had very straight, elegant backs, golden wings and she noticed their feet were turned out as they walked. Surely it couldn't be! She turned to Lexa and Nanny Pearl to get their attention but they were in deep discussion about where the parasols for the first act of the ballet were to be kept. By the time she turned back the fairies were gone. Ruby shook her head and decided she must have been mistaken and in she went to get ready for the show.

Chapter Fourteen

Ruby in Wonderland

The ballet school had doubled in size for the day. A twenty four hour spell to add what seemed like a rabbit warren of changing rooms had meant there was space for everyone to get ready. Nanny Pearl and Lexa went off to find Hilaria. Ruby looked on the notice board in search of her dressing room number. She found her name and smiled. She was sharing with Flint and Coral – perfect!

Ruby found the empty dressing room surprising quickly and unpacked her ballet bag on one of the three dressing tables. The Alice band took pride of place in the centre and she unpacked her bag and laid everything out neatly. The costumes were already hanging up on three hooks on the back wall.

In came Flint quickly followed by Coral. They chattered excitedly as they got ready, helping each other with their costumes and checking for any hair out of place. Ruby put on her Alice band and Coral helped to pin it into position.

"All students to the stage please!" Shouted a speaker high up in the corner of the room. "Costume check and warm up on stage, quickly please."

The stage was full of restless fairies fiddling with their colourful costumes. The curtains were closed. Hilaria led the warm up exercises and inspected all their costumes.

"Get to your positions please. And make sure the correct props are ready Pearlie darling!" Hilaria called into the wings at a grinning Nanny Pearl, clipboard in hand. She continued. "You are all extremely talented! Concentration heads on and enjoy yourselves!" Nanny Pearl blew Ruby a kiss from the wings as Ruby practiced her leap one more time on the stage.

The sound of footsteps, laughing, jabbering, sweet wrappers crackling, children screeching and phones beeping could all be heard from behind the closed red curtains. It sounded like the theatre audience was very full. Lexa and Jasper should be in their seats by now, Ruby thought.

It was time for the ballet to begin and the audience went quiet apart from Coral's baby sister shouting "Where's Coral, I want Coral!" Her father whispered to her and she quietened down.

The music began, the curtains opened and Ruby danced onto the stage. She sat down and acted reading her book with her toes pointed neatly in front of her. Across the floor ran Coral in her white rabbit costume looking very concerned about the time on her oversized pocket watch. Ruby was captivated by Coral's dancing, her every step was better than Ruby had ever seen her dance in rehearsal. Ruby was so wrapped up in watching Coral that she nearly forgot to get up and follow her down the rabbit hole. Luckily the music reminded Ruby of exactly what to do and she danced across the stage just as she had practiced so many times before.

There was huge applause when the scene ended and the dancers silently hugged in the wings and got ready to continue.

"Keep it up everyone, you're performing so well." whispered Hilaria.

The whole ballet went without a hitch apart from when one of the flowers turned the wrong way and bumped into her friend. The friend proceeded to tell her off much to the audience's glee. They were only three and a half and looked so cute that the whole audience burst into laughter. Grumpy fairy flowers are really quite adorable!

The Mad Hatter's tea party was wonderfully bonkers. The cards were hilarious and fell over exactly when they should. Much to Hilaria's relief and delight.

AND…

Ruby's grand jeté, THE grand jeté that had worried her so much was a success. It felt graceful, she thought, a good split and she landed well too. In fact it looked amazing, it really did. There was even a gasp from the audience and Ruby was convinced she heard someone sounding very much like Lexa shout "YES!"

At the end all the dancers piled onto the stage to bow and curtsey. The theatre erupted into cheers of "Encore! Bravo! Stupendous! Tremendous! What staging! Wow and only a school production! What a great future these dancers have! More!"

Ruby and her friends were grinning from ear to ear. Their hard work had been worth it. They had poured their hearts and souls into the performance and they had loved every minute.

Hilaria walked onto the stage "Thank you all for coming! Well done everyone, you worked so hard. I am very proud of each and every one of you and I am honoured to call you my students."

"I have a little surprise for you!" Hilaria raised her left arm beckoning two extremely famous dancers onto the stage. Ruby gasped as did almost everyone else. Nanny Pearl smiled a knowing smile from the wings. She had planned this all along!

Francesca Houseflower and Steven McSunbeam walked onto the stage. Yes them, the actual, real live, dancers. Ruby jumped up and down and squealed with delight and her ears started to fizz and…. POP out flew ribbons of rainbow glitter, showing shapes of dancers pirouetting around her head.

Francesca and Steven walked to the front of the stage and turned round to face the students. They started to clap and the audience stood up and joined in. It lasted a good several minutes but finally Francesca raised her hand to ask for quiet so she could speak.

When the clapping died down Francesca spoke. "It is wonderful to see so much talent on stage today. Such attention to detail at this age will reap rewards in the future. The world is out there for you to conquer!" Francesca smiled and nodded at Ruby. Ruby touched her Alice band affectionately and her smile grew so huge it that almost reached ears.

Steven took over. "And now we are honoured to dance for you. We will dance a pas de deux from La Féerie Mal Gardée. A ballet by Sir Kenny Macaroons and I believe one of Hilaria's favourite." Steven looked towards Hilaria who clasped her hands, smiled and nodded thankfully. He continued. "The Royal Ethereal Ballet will perform this in the autumn and we have tickets for everyone here today to come and see us!"

Well that was it, the fairy ballerina students flew up into the air, their ears were popping and multi-coloured glitter filled the theatre! It took several minutes for Hilaria to calm them all down and get everyone off the stage to watch the performance but eventually all was very quiet.

The lights dimmed. The music began. Steven McSunbeam and Francesca Houseflower stepped onto the stage and started to dance. They moved from one elegant pose to the next, balancing, spinning and leaping. The magical movements and graceful shapes on stage had the audience mesmerised. Ruby studied every single perfect step the dancers made. She fiddled absentmindedly with her ruby necklace and turned to Flint and whispered.

"One day that will be us!"

Thank yous!

To Jenny for the most wonderful drawings that bring my words to life.
To Nige for helping edit the book, always making me laugh and putting up with me.
To my beautiful mum for her never ending love, support and faith in my abilities.
To Jacob for letting me read him the story even though he's not too keen on ballet and would have preferred that the fairies ate burgers!
To Caroline and Paul for also helping with the edit and being jolly good sorts.
To dad – thank you for loving the theatre. I like to think you would have been proud.
To Beano – we miss you stinky dog!
And finally to everyone I teach for making my life a joy!

About the author:

Hilary is a ballet teacher who lives in Sussex by the sea. In order to raise money for her ballet school's summer show Hilary decided to write a book about Fairy Ballerinas. The teacher's name in this book is Hilaria Tiptoes but some suspect she is writing about herself!

23119174R00040

Printed in Poland
by Amazon Fulfillment
Poland Sp. z o.o., Wrocław